Dear Parents:

Congratulations! Your child is taking the first steps on an exciting journey. The destination? Independent reading!

STEP INTO READING® will help your child get there. The program offers five steps to reading success. Each step includes fun stories and colorful art or photographs. In addition to original fiction and books with favorite characters, there are Step into Reading Non-Fiction Readers, Phonics Readers and Boxed Sets, Sticker Readers, and Comic Readers—a complete literacy program with something to interest every child.

Learning to Read, Step by Step!

Ready to Read Preschool–Kindergarten
• big type and easy words • rhyme and rhythm • picture clues
For children who know the alphabet and are eager to begin reading.

Reading with Help Preschool–Grade 1
• basic vocabulary • short sentences • simple stories
For children who recognize familiar words and sound out new words with help.

Reading on Your Own Grades 1–3
• engaging characters • easy-to-follow plots • popular topics
For children who are ready to read on their own.

Reading Paragraphs Grades 2–3
• challenging vocabulary • short paragraphs • exciting stories
For newly independent readers who read simple sentences with confidence.

Ready for Chapters Grades 2–4
• chapters • longer paragraphs • full-color art
For children who want to take the plunge into chapter books but still like colorful pictures.

STEP INTO READING® is designed to give every child a successful reading experience. The grade levels are only guides; children will progress through the steps at their own speed, developing confidence in their reading.

Remember, a lifetime love of reading starts with a single step!

Copyright © 2015 Disney Enterprises, Inc., and Pixar Animation Studios. All rights reserved.
Published in the United States by Random House Children's Books, a division of Penguin Random House LLC, 1745 Broadway, New York, NY 10019, and in Canada by Random House of Canada, a division of Penguin Random House Ltd., Toronto, in conjunction with Disney Enterprises, Inc.

Step into Reading, Random House, and the Random House colophon are registered trademarks of Penguin Random House LLC.

Visit us on the Web!
StepIntoReading.com
randomhousekids.com

Educators and librarians, for a variety of teaching tools, visit us at RHTeachersLibrarians.com

ISBN 978-0-7364-3316-7 (trade) — ISBN 978-0-7364-8169-4 (lib. bdg.) — ISBN 978-0-7364-3317-4 (ebook)

Printed in the United States of America   10 9 8 7 6 5 4 3 2 1

DISNEY · PIXAR

INSIDE OUT

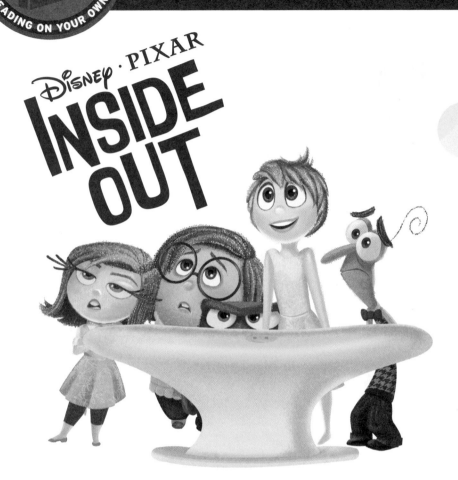

JOURNEY into the MIND

By Melissa Lagonegro

Illustrated by the Disney Storybook Art Team

Random House 🏠 New York

This is Headquarters.
It is in Riley's mind.
Riley is eleven years old.
Her mind is filled
with different Emotions.
They take care of her.

Joy is an Emotion.
Her job is
to keep Riley happy.
Joy wants Riley
to have happy core memories.
Happy memories are yellow.

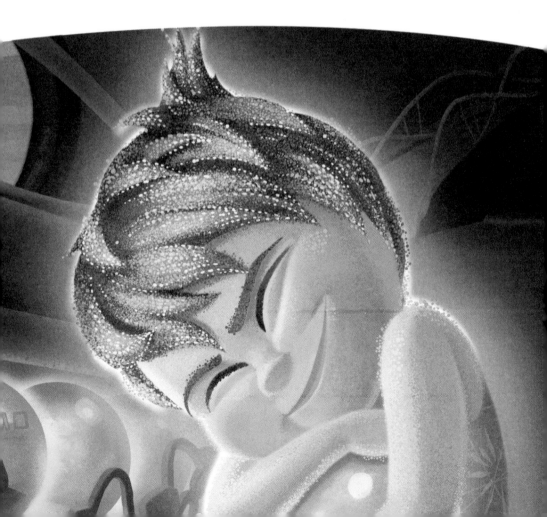

Fear is another Emotion.
He makes sure Riley is safe.
Disgust keeps Riley away
from gross things.

Anger stands up for Riley.
Nobody knows what Sadness does.
Sadness is gloomy and slow.
Riley is always unhappy
when Sadness is in control.

Core memories power
Riley's Islands of Personality.
There is Family Island,
Honesty Island,
and Hockey Island.

Riley also has
Friendship Island
and Goofball Island.
These islands make Riley
who she is.

The Emotions are shocked when
Riley's family moves
to San Francisco.
They don't know what to do.

Sadness touches a happy memory.
It turns blue
and becomes a sad memory.
Joy must stop Sadness
from touching more
happy memories.

Riley does not like
San Francisco.
The Emotions are worried.
Joy tries to stay positive
and calm them down.

Riley goes to a new school.

She meets her class.

Sadness takes over.

Riley starts to cry.

Joy does not like it

when Riley cries.

Joy tries to stop Sadness.
Joy and Sadness both get sucked
out of Headquarters.

Riley's core memories
go with them!
Anger, Fear, and Disgust are
in charge of Headquarters now!

At dinner that night,
Riley is not happy.
She cannot have happy thoughts
without Joy and her core memories.

Riley is angry.
She is rude to her parents.
They send her
to her room.

Goofball Island crumbles
into the Memory Dump.
Nothing comes back
from the Memory Dump.
Joy and Sadness need to get back
to Headquarters quickly!

After dinner,

Riley talks to her friend Meg.

Meg tells her she has a new friend.

Riley gets upset.

Friendship Island crumbles!

When Riley was little,
she had an imaginary friend
named Bing Bong.

Joy and Sadness meet him.
He can help them get back
to Headquarters.

Riley tries out
for the hockey team.
Without her core memories,
she misses the puck and falls!
Hockey Island crumbles!

Bing Bong is sad.

Riley has forgotten about him.

He cries candy.

Sadness talks to Bing Bong.

She makes him feel better.

Anger wants Riley to go back
to her old home
to make new memories.
Riley decides to run away.

Joy, Bing Bong, and Sadness try
to get back to Headquarters.
Joy and Bing Bong fall
into the Memory Dump!
Sadness is alone.

Joy realizes she has been wrong
about Sadness all along.
Riley needs Sadness
to help her feel sad
before she can be happy again.

Joy needs to find Sadness.
Bing Bong helps her get
out of the Memory Dump.

Joy finds Sadness.
They bounce on a trampoline
and get back to Headquarters!

Joy lets Sadness take control.
Sadness helps Riley
feel really sad.
Riley realizes she does not
want to run away.
She goes back to her parents.

Riley tells her parents
that she misses her old home.
Her parents let her know
that it is okay to feel sad.
They hug.

Now all the Emotions work
together in Headquarters
to help Riley.